Friends forever

by Pippa Goodhart

illustrated by Ailie Busby

This book is dedicated to
Ethan James Lang
and Bethany Scarlet Lang.
Our precious gifts.
Love,
Mum and Dad.

First published in Great Britain 2003
by Egmont Books Limited
239 Kensington High Street, London W8 6SA

Text copyright © 2003 Pippa Goodhart
Illustration copyright © 2003 Ailie Busby

The moral rights of the author and illustrator have been asserted

ISBN 1 4052 0408 7

10 9 8 7 6 5 4 3 2 1

A CIP catalogue record for this title is available from the British Library

Printed and bound in Great Britain
by Cox & Wyman Ltd, Reading, Berkshire

Contents

1 Family Fruit

In the playground, Maxine told Minnie, 'Mrs Dobbs said that we're going to make trees after lunch.'

'You don't make trees. You grow them,' said Minnie. 'And it takes years and years for them to grow big.'

'Well, this kind of tree must be quicker,' said Maxine.

The end of playtime bell rang and Maxine whizzed her wheelchair to get to the door first, with Minnie running to keep up.

1

'Now,' said Mrs Dobbs, 'as part of our history work, we are going to make family trees.'

'Told you!' whispered Maxine. But Minnie was right too.

Mrs Dobbs explained, 'A family tree is a kind of diagram showing the shape of your family. You put your own name at the bottom of the paper. Then you put lines reaching up to your mother's and father's names. More lines reach up to the names of their mothers and fathers. Do you see?' She was drawing on the board. 'As you go back in time you have more lines and more people. That's why it looks like a tree.'

'I think it looks more like a bush than a tree,' whispered Maxine.

Mrs Dobbs told them, 'I want you all to draw your own family trees, back to the time of Queen Victoria. We are going to be working on the Victorians this term and it will be interesting to know about your family in those days. Victorian times were more than a hundred years ago. You'll need to ask your parents for help. See how far back you can go. Now, Minnie, please could you hand everybody a clean sheet of paper, and then you can begin.'

Maxine began her family tree straight away. She wrote *Maxine* in big bold letters at the bottom of her piece of paper. She added her brothers, Darrel and Ben and Bobo, and her sister Sarah in slightly smaller letters beside her name. She drew a picture of herself, scribbling her hair with an orange crayon.

'Why haven't you started yours?' she asked Minnie.

'I'm thinking,' said Minnie. Minnie picked up her pencil and carefully wrote

Minnie, very small, on a bottom corner of her paper.

'That's wrong,' said Maxine.

'No it's not,' said Minnie. 'It's right for me because I've only got my Mum. I haven't got a dad.'

Minnie drew herself with neat straight brown hair, and Sootica, her little black cat, beside her.

'I want you to finish off your family trees at home,' said Mrs Dobbs.

'Shall we do ours together?' said Maxine.

'Yes. You come to my house after school,' said Minnie. 'Mum said that there would be a surprise waiting when I got home.'

Maxine and Minnie lived next door to

4

each other. Sometimes they went to Maxine's house because it was full of people and animals and there were always things going on. But it wasn't a good place for doing homework. Minnie's house was quieter and there was usually room on the kitchen table.

When they got to Minnie's house, they found an old lady sitting on a deckchair in the front garden. The old lady was the surprise. Minnie's mum told them, 'This is my Auntie Dot. She's Minnie's *Great* Auntie Dot, and she's come to stay for a few days.'

'Hello, Minnie my dear,' said Great Auntie Dot. 'I'm very pleased to meet you.'

Minnie felt a little shy of the lady who offered a knobbly old hand to shake. But she said, 'Hello,' and shook the hand. It was warm and nice. Then she pointed to Maxine. 'Maxine lives next door. She's my best friend.'

'Lucky you!' said Great Auntie Dot with a smile. 'Having a best friend is the most wonderful thing in the world. I had a best friend when I was your age. She was called Joan. We used to make dens together, and we wrote letters to each other in our own secret code.'

'Where's Joan now?' asked Maxine.

Great Auntie Dot made a face and

sighed, 'We went our different ways after school and we lost touch.'

Minnie said, 'Maxine and I are going to be friends for ever.'

'Good for you!' said Great Auntie Dot, and Minnie decided that she liked her.

After tea, Maxine and Minnie spread their homework out on the table.

'What's that you're doing?' asked Great Auntie Dot.

'It's our family trees,' said Maxine.

Minnie's mum explained, 'They've got to find out who was in their families in Victorian times.'

'Oh, I can help them with that,' said Great Auntie Dot. 'At least I can help Minnie with the people on my side of the family. And I could show you a way to make your family tree look as if it's very ancient, if you'd like that, Maxine?'

'Yes, please! How do you do it?'

'With the last splash of tea left in this pot.' Great Auntie Dot turned to Minnie's mum, 'Carol, is there an old tray that we could use?'

Rolling up her sleeves, Great Auntie Dot set to work. She showed Maxine how to tear carefully around the sheet of paper to make it look tatty-old. Then she poured cold tea into a shallow tray and put the paper into it.

'Won't it get soggy and fall to bits?' asked Maxine.

'Not if we're careful.' The white paper turned a blotchy brown tea colour. 'It's got to be left somewhere flat to dry,' said Great Auntie Dot. She carefully lifted the wet paper out of the tea and laid it down on the draining board beside the sink. 'You won't be able to do any more work on it tonight,' she told Maxine. 'So, what shall we do now?'

'Please could you tell us about the olden days?' asked Minnie.

'Well, I can tell you about the olden days when I was young. That was during the Second World War,' said Great Auntie Dot. 'In those days, we hardly ever got new clothes or sweets. We only got a very little of any of the nice things to eat. It was a dull time in many ways, except for the times

9

when we were frightened.'

'Frightened of what?' asked Minnie.

'Frightened that the enemy might come and drop bombs on our houses. But most of all, we were frightened for our fathers who were away fighting in the war.'

'Was your father away?'

'He was,' said Great Auntie Dot. 'He was your great-grandfather, Minnie, and he was in the army. So I was a bit like you, living with just my mother and my sister at home.'

'Did your dad come back?' asked Maxine.

Great Auntie Dot shook her head sadly. 'No, I'm afraid that he was killed,' she said.

'Poor him. Poor you,' said Maxine.

'Thank you,' said Great Auntie Dot, then she smiled. 'Still, Victorians were a

10

long time before all that. They came before I was born.'

'Wow!' said Maxine.

Great Auntie Dot laughed. 'But I used to talk with my old granny just the way that you and I are talking now, and Granny told me what it had been like when she was young.'

'Was she Victorian?' asked Minnie.

'She was,' said Great Auntie Dot. 'I can even show you what she looked like because I've got a photograph of her in my locket. She left the locket for me to remember her by when she died. Would you like to see?'

'Yes please,' said Maxine and Minnie together.

Great Auntie Dot reached for a silver oval that hung from a silver chain around her neck, and she opened it out. Inside the locket was a brown and cream

photograph of a girl with a big ribbon on one side of her hair and a rather cross look on her face. 'Minnie, my dear, that girl in the photograph is your great-great-granny, who wasn't a granny at all when this picture was taken, of course. She was only a little older than you are now.'

'What was she called?' asked Minnie.

'She was called Dorothy, and I was named after her. Dot is short for Dorothy.'

'She looks a bit grumpy,' said Minnie,

12

and Great Auntie Dot laughed again.

'Not a bit of it!' she said. 'She was one of the funniest, most laughing people I ever met. But in those days, it took seven minutes of sitting perfectly still to make a photograph. You can't keep a real smile going for that long.'

'I could!' said Maxine.

'Really?' said Great Auntie Dot. 'Let's test you. I'll time the two of you. Now, keep perfectly still and smile. Ready . . . go!' and she pushed a button on her watch.

Maxine and Minnie smiled wide and tried to keep still. But time seems to go very slowly when there is nothing to do but keep completely still. Minnie's mum made faces at them. The sides of Maxine's and Minnie's mouths began to ache and then they began to wobble. Then they looked at each other and they

13

began to laugh out loud.

'Hopeless!' said Great Auntie Dot. 'You only lasted seventy seconds!'

When Maxine went home, Minnie had Great Auntie Dot to herself. Great Auntie Dot helped her to write down the names of her mum and her mum's mum and dad.

'That's Gran and Grandad,' said Minnie.

'That's right. Their names are Susan and Douglas,' said Great Auntie Dot. 'Susan is my little sister.' Then she told Minnie about Susan's mother and father, and their parents.

'Can aunts be part of the tree too?'

asked Minnie. 'I'd like to put you in.' She drew a sideways line and wrote Dot. 'Now my family tree has got another branch.'

'Oh, nothing so grand,' said Great Auntie Dot. 'I think I'm just a twig.'

'A fruit on a twig,' said Minnie, and that gave her an idea. She got pens and carefully coloured the trunk and branches and twigs of her family tree brown. Then she got red and green and purple and orange and yellow and she drew fruit shapes around all the names of the people who were on her tree.

'Very nice,' said Great Auntie Dot. 'I like being a cherry!'

It was a fun evening, talking to Great Auntie Dot and working on her family tree, but at bedtime Minnie was rather sad and quiet.

'What's up with you?' asked her mother

as they had their goodnight cuddle.

'There's a bit missing on my family tree,' said Minnie.

'Which bit is that?' asked her mum.

'The bit where my dad and his family should be,' said Minnie.

'Ah,' said Minnie's mum. Minnie looked at her.

'Why haven't I ever had a dad?'

'Minnie, my love, you have had a dad. Everyone has a father or they couldn't exist.'

Minnie was about to say something else, but her mum put a finger onto Minnie's lips. 'I will tell you all about your father, Min, but not just now. You're tired and I'm tired and I must go and see that Great Auntie Dot is happy downstairs. But I promise, truly promise, that when we get some time together, then I will tell you.'

So Minnie drew a stump of branch squashed on to the paper beside her mum's name. The branch didn't have any name or fruit on it. Soon it will, thought Minnie. Soon I'll know all about my dad.

2 A Posh Lady and her Maid

Maxine and Minnie knew that today was going to be special. Mrs Dobbs had told the class, 'It will be like going back in time. You will have a whole school day of living like Victorians.'

'I think that I'm going to like being a Victorian,' said Minnie, as she put one of Great Auntie Dot's headscarves around her shoulders.

'What's that scarf for?' asked Maxine.

'It's being a shawl,' said Minnie. 'I wish I had a mob cap like yours.'

Maxine touched her white cap. 'I think it looks like the lid on a mince

pie,' she said.

Great Auntie Dot waved Maxine and
Minnie off to school. 'Have a lovely time,
girls,' she said. 'Mind you don't get
blown over!'

'Blown over?' said Maxine. 'What does
she mean?'

'It's something she told me about
Victorian clothes,' said Minnie as she
tugged at the long skirt that was tangling
around her legs. 'She said that her granny
once saw a very grand lady blown over
by the wind. The lady was wearing one

19

of those great big skirts called a crinoline. Great Auntie Dot said it was as big as a tent. Anyway, the wind got under the skirt and pushed the lady over! And Great Auntie Dot's granny saw the lady's bloomers and everything!'

'What did she do?' asked Maxine.

'She helped the lady get up again. Then the lady gave her a penny with Queen Victoria's head on it.'

'What if that happens to Mrs Dobbs today!' said Maxine. 'Do you think that Mrs Dobbs will be wearing bloomers?'

'Don't be mean!' said Minnie.

But Minnie began to feel less kindly towards Mrs Dobbs when she and Maxine got to school.

Mrs Dobbs was waiting for the children at the classroom door. She was wearing a long skirt, but it didn't stick out or look like a tent. Her hair was in a bun and she had a big bell in her hand.

'Line up!' she told the children in a strict voice. Minnie ran up to Mrs Dobbs.

'Mrs Dobbs,' she said. 'My Great Auntie Dot's told me some things about Victorians. Shall I tell you about a lady with a big skirt?' But Mrs Dobbs scowled down at Minnie.

'Minnie Brown, will

you please take your place in the line. There will be no talking!'

Minnie felt a little frightened. She scuttled to get in line. She wasn't used to being told off. It was a horrid feeling. Minnie whispered to Maxine, 'I don't think I'm going to like being Victorian after all.' And suddenly Mrs Dobbs was in front of her and with a finger pointing.

'Minnie Brown, go right to the back of the line. I said that there was to be no talking!'

'I'll come with you,' said Maxine.

Mrs Dobbs was still very strict when they went into the classroom. She looked at everybody's hands and she told Maxine off for having dirt on hers. She even pretended to hit Maxine's hand with a ruler.

'She's being horrible!' said Minnie, but Maxine just laughed. Maxine thought it was funny when Mrs Dobbs made them all sit with their hands behind the backs of their chairs as she took the register.

Then Mrs Dobbs smiled her normal Mrs Dobbs smile at them all.

'I'm sorry if I frightened some of you as we came in,' she said. 'But I wanted you to know what it might have been like, coming to school in Victorian times.'

'I knew you were only pretending,' said Maxine.

Well, I didn't, thought Minnie. 'Please can I sit next to you on the coach?' she asked Maxine.

Maxine and Minnie sat right at the front of the coach on the way to Lucus Hall and Maxine chattered all the way. 'Mrs Dobbs told me something, Min. She said that in Victorian days it was only rich people who got a wheelchair when they needed to have one. She said a poor

girl who couldn't walk would have had to sit in one place or be carried by somebody strong. She couldn't go anywhere on her own.'

'Poor her,' said Minnie.

'Yes,' said Maxine. 'So that means I've got to be a posh person today.'

'Why?'

'Because I have got a wheelchair, of course. Hey, Min, let's pretend that we're real Victorian people with names and everything!'

'OK,' said Minnie. 'Who will you be, then?'

Maxine thought for a moment. 'I think I'll be some grand lord and lady's daughter. I'll be Lady Roseanna Higginpot. You'll have to be my servant. You can wear my mob cap, if you like. A lady wouldn't wear one of those. It's your job to push me around and look after me. You can be called Martha.'

'But you don't need pushing,' said Minnie.

'In Victorian days I would,' said Maxine. 'We want to be properly Victorian.'

Maxine started being grand straight away. 'Pass me the crisps from my lunch box, maid.'

'Crisps aren't Victorian,' said Minnie, but she got them out of Maxine's bag and handed them over.

At Lucus Hall there was a man with whiskers down the sides of his face who told the children about how things were done in the kitchen of a grand Victorian house. He said that they could all have turns, washing rags in a tub and then putting them through a mangle to get the water out.

'Mind those fingers,' said Mrs Dobbs.

Minnie scrubbed floors and carried a bucket of coal and rubbed black stuff on the stove.

Maxine told Minnie, 'You'll have to do my jobs because you're my servant.' So Minnie used the heavy iron to flatten the cloths and she polished pans, even though those were meant to be Maxine's jobs.

'You should pay me,' said Minnie.

'I might give you a penny like that posh lady who got blown over,' said Maxine, and then she yawned. 'Actually,' she said, 'it's a bit boring being posh and just watching everybody else work.'

'Well, you do some of the work then!' said Minnie, who was getting hot and cross. Everything Victorian seemed to be very heavy and it was a warm day.

Maxine still liked the idea of being grand and important. 'I don't think that's shiny enough,' she told Minnie. 'You'd better do that one again.'

'Don't be so bossy!' said Minnie, but it was time to stop anyway.

Mrs Dobbs clapped her hands and said, 'It's lunchtime. Everybody follow me to the meadow for our picnic.' And off she went and all the children followed.

Maxine told Minnie. 'Push me to the meadow, maid.'

But Minnie folded her arms. 'No!' she said.

'You've got to push me,' said Maxine. 'Servants have to serve.' She turned to the man with whiskers and she asked him, 'Didn't servants have to do what the rich people told them to do in Victorian days?'

'They did,' he agreed. Minnie scowled. 'Well, this

servant is going to serve you right!' she said, and she ran up the step and after the others to the meadow.

Mrs Dobbs's class sat on the cool grass under some trees. They were all chatting and opening their pack lunches, all except Minnie who kept looking back towards the house. Mrs Dobbs came over and asked her, 'Minnie, where's Maxine?'

Minnie's mouth began to quiver. 'I've lost her,' she said.

'Lost Maxine!' said Mrs Dobbs. 'How could anybody lose something as bright and noisy as Maxine Higgins? Where did you lose her?'

Tears were running down Minnie's face. 'In the kitchen,' she said. 'Maxine was being bossy, so I left her. There was a step. I think she's stuck there.'

'Then we'd better hurry and find her,' said Mrs Dobbs, and she and Minnie set off, running, towards the house.

They found Maxine still in the kitchen with the man with big whiskers. He winked at Mrs Dobbs and said, 'Have you come for young Lady Roseanna Higginpot, ma'am? She seems to think that she should be sitting on the grass in the meadow with the servants. But I've told her that isn't appropriate for a young lady of the nobility. She should dine in the Great Hall with her mama and papa and not speak until she's spoken to.'

'But I don't want . . .' began Maxine. She looked more worried now than she did when Mrs Dobbs was pretending to hit her hand with a ruler.

Minnie tugged at the sleeve of the man with whiskers. 'She's not really posh in real life. She's my friend Maxine and we were just pretending.'

'That's right,' said Mrs Dobbs. 'And I think that it's time to go back to being the real Maxine Higgins now. Shall we join the others in the meadow?'

On the coach going home, Minnie had an idea.

'You know what, Max?' she said.

'What?' asked Maxine.

'I didn't like being a servant. Perhaps that's because in real true life I'm the one who's posh, but I just don't know it yet.'

'How do you mean?'

'Well, my dad might be anybody. He could even be royal or something.'

'Wow, yes,' said Maxine. 'Your dad

might be a king who fell in love with your beautiful mother. But he wasn't allowed to marry your mum because he had to marry some horrible princess. Wow, Min! Ask your mum and find out!'

'I have,' said Minnie. 'She's going to tell me.'

'Brilliant!' said Maxine, but Minnie wasn't so sure. What if her dad really *was* a king? She looked out of the window and wondered.

3 Poor Orphans

On Saturday morning Maxine asked Minnie, 'What do you want to play?'

'Anything,' said Minnie. 'Just so long as it isn't you being a posh person and me being the servant having to look after you. I know, let's both be poor orphans with nobody at all to look after us.'

'OK, we'll pretend we've got no mum or dad or anybody, and nowhere to live.'

'Perhaps we could make a den, like Great Auntie Dot did with her best friend Joan,' said Minnie.

Maxine laughed. 'I can't imagine your Great Auntie Dot as a little girl. Can you?'

'Well, she was one,' said Minnie. 'And in years and years and years I suppose that we'll both be old ladies like her.'

Maxine's garden was full of plants and trees and swings and bikes and a sandpit. It had a deep hedge at the far end of it.

'There's a place we can push right inside the hedge and make a den,' Maxine told Minnie. 'We can camouflage it so that our enemies don't find us.'

'What enemies?' asked Minnie.

'I don't know yet,' said Maxine. 'I'll think of some.'

By pushing branches aside and breaking off some bits of twig, Maxine and Minnie made the hole in the hedge big enough for both of them.

'I'll find us some furniture,' said
Minnie. She found two little logs from
the woodpile for them to sit on.

'Where will we sleep?' asked Minnie.

'I think we only need room for one of
us to lie down,' said Maxine. 'We'll have
to take turns to be on guard.'

'In case our enemies come,' said Minnie.

Maxine's mum found them a
waterproof plastic sheet that used to go

35

at the bottom of a tent. She let them use an old baby blanket too.

Maxine and Minnie rummaged in Maxine's big dressing-up box. They pulled on ragged clothes that made them feel old-fashioned and poor. Then they went to live in their den.

'What are we going to eat?' asked Maxine. 'I'm starving already.'

'Is there any food in the garden?' asked Minnie. 'The apples on the tree in my garden are too small and hard.'

'We might have to eat them anyway,' said Maxine. 'Either that or starve.'

'I'm not hungry yet,' said Minnie. 'I'm just thirsty. We could get some cartons of juice from my mum.'

'Orphans don't get given cartons of juice!' said Maxine. 'They have to find things to eat and drink. Tell you what,' she said, 'we could be so dying of thirst

that we sneak into the castle of the Dreaded Queen and steal some water from the Dreaded Queen's tap without her catching us.'

'Yes,' whispered Minnie. 'The Dreaded Queen wants to catch us to be her slave-servants. She killed our parents and that's why we're orphans. That's why we don't care about stealing from her.'

Maxine sat guard. 'I'll give a signal if there's danger,' she told Minnie.

Minnie crouched down low and crept,

quiet as a mouse, to the back door of Maxine's house. Then she stopped still. The Dreaded Queen was in there, cooking. Probably boiled babies, thought Minnie, although it smelt more like cake. But Minnie couldn't get past the Dreaded Queen to the water tap, so she signalled to Maxine that she was going to try her house instead.

'I'm going to the House of Dragons!' she mouthed.

'I'll keep guarding the den,' Maxine whispered back. 'Be quick!'

Minnie peeped around to make sure that nobody was looking. Then she ran as fast as she could in her ragged clothes and bare feet over the gravel, round the front from Maxine's house to hers. She crept quietly through the gate into her garden and tiptoed up to the back door. It was open, so she slipped inside and

reached for a couple of plastic cups. Then she heard footsteps coming! Minnie's heart beat fast and her mind whizzed. Quick as she could, she slipped behind the door and tried not to move or breath too loudly as her mum and Great Auntie Dot came into the room. Minnie heard Great Auntie Dot pull out a chair and sit down while her mother switched the kettle on.

'Coffee?' said Minnie's mum.

'That would be nice,' said Great Auntie Dot. 'And then you must decide what you are going to do about your problem with Minnie.'

Minnie, behind the door, wanted to ask, 'what problem with me?', but she was meant to be keeping secret from the Dragons. Besides, she wanted to hear more of what they had to say.

Minnie's mum said, 'I must tell Minnie everything.'

'You really should,' agreed Great

Auntie Dot. 'After all, it is such a wonderful story.'

'Would you like a biscuit?' asked Minnie's mum, and Minnie bit her lip, wishing that they would go back to talking about the 'wonderful story'. But they didn't.

There was the sound of the milk being put back into the fridge and the biscuit tin being opened and closed, and then Minnie heard her mum and Great Auntie Dot go out of the kitchen.

Minnie waited a moment to be sure that nobody was coming back, and then, quick as a fish, she darted to the table and helped herself to two biscuits, and ran out of the door and back round to Maxine's garden and the den.

'You've been ages!' said Maxine.

'I got stuck,' said Minnie. 'Mum and . . . I mean the Dragons came in and nearly caught me, but I've got us each a biscuit.'

'Well done,' said Maxine. 'And I saw two panthers, but I stayed very still and they went away.' Minnie knew that the panthers were really Maxine's big black cat, Blackie, and her own little Sootica.

Maxine had a stick in her hand. 'We need to guard against wild animals as well as people enemies, Min. We really need a door. And we need to make the shelter waterproof in case it rains, although it's so hot I don't think it'll ever rain again.' Maxine wiped a hand over her hot face. 'Hey, Min, what about the drink you were going to get?'

'Oh, dear. I forgot about it,' said Minnie. 'Sorry.'

'I'm so thirsty I could drink the sea,' said Maxine. 'But I suppose that's an orphan kind of thing to feel. I don't think I've ever felt really really thirsty before.'

But Minnie wasn't listening to Maxine. She was gazing at nothing. Maxine waved a hand in front of her face. 'What are you thinking about, Min?'

'Something the Dragons said,' said Minnie. 'Mum and Great Auntie Dot were talking about telling me something. It sounded like something really important. I think it might be about my dad.'

'Wow!' said Maxine. 'What did they say?' Minnie shrugged.

'Nothing much, except that Great Auntie Dot said that it was a wonderful story.'

'Double wow!' said Maxine. She grabbed hold of Minnie's arm. 'I bet I know what it is, Min. If it's a wonderful story, then your dad must really be a prince or a king or something. Or, if he's dead, then you are half a real orphan in true life! Or . . .'

'I hope he isn't dead,' said Minnie. She thought of Great Auntie Dot's father not coming back from the war.

'But it wouldn't make any difference for you,' said Maxine. 'You've never had your dad, so why would you be sad if he was dead?'

'I just would,' said Minnie. She felt sad now, thinking about it. 'Can we play a different game now?'

'Or,' said Maxine, waving her hands around, 'maybe he isn't dead and you can go and find him and he's soooo rich he can buy you anything you want! You could get jewels and a big house and servants. It'd be great!'

'Then I'd have to move away from here,' said Minnie. 'I like living here with Mum, and having you next door.' Minnie didn't think that she wanted any big change in her life at all. 'And I don't

want servants. And I don't want to be an orphan either.'

'Then let's just be us again and get a drink from my mum. I think she might be cooking buns,' said Maxine. 'I smelt them.'

'So did I,' said Minnie. 'And, Max?'

'Yes?'

'Will you stay friends with me, whatever my dad is and whoever I am?'

'Of course I will, silly!' said Maxine.

4 Somebody Special

It was Great Auntie Dot's last day at Minnie's house, and it was still sunny and hot. Maxine and Minnie were making patchwork ice cubes.

'What in the world are patchwork ice cubes?' asked Great Auntie Dot.

'They're like normal ice cubes to make your drink cold,' said Maxine. 'But they're prettier. Look.' She carefully poured orange juice into three of the little squares in an ice cube tray.

'I'm doing the purple,' explained

46

Minnie. 'Blackcurrant juice.' She poured purple drink into three other cubes.

'And you can use food colouring to make water blue and green and yellow and anything you like,' explained Maxine.

'How jolly!' said Great Auntie Dot.

'But they take ages and ages to turn into hard ice,' said Minnie. 'And I need cooling down now.'

'Oh, so do I,' said Great Auntie Dot. 'And as it happens, I've got an idea for something we could make to cool ourselves with straight away.'

'What's that?' asked Minnie.

'Fans. Fetch me some paper and sticky tape, Minnie, and I'll show you what to do.'

Great Auntie Dot showed Maxine and Minnie how to fold the paper over and over, until it was all zigzagged on top of itself. 'Like a concertina,' said Great

Auntie Dot. 'And if you tape it together at one end and open out the other, you've got a fan.' Great Auntie Dot fanned herself like a posh lady. 'A gentle breeze. That's better!' she said.

Minnie drew flowers and stars and butterflies on a piece of paper and folded it into a fan.

Maxine folded plain paper and coloured it with red and blue stripes for her fan. When you looked at it from the left, it seemed as if it was all red, and when you looked from the right, it seemed all blue.

'Stand in front and I'll fan it very fast,' said Maxine.

'Now it looks purple,' said Minnie.

'Very clever,' said Great Auntie

Dot. 'But I've just had an even better idea for cooling us down.'

'What's that?' asked Maxine and Minnie.

'A trip to the seaside! How would you all like to have a ride in my car to see the sea?'

'Brilliant!' shouted Maxine.

'Oh, yes, please!' said Minnie.

Minnie and her mum packed up sandwiches and drinks and swimming costumes and towels and sun cream while Maxine went to ask if she was allowed to go with them.

They put a folding chair for Great Auntie Dot together with Maxine's wheelchair into the back of Great Auntie Dot's car. Then they set off for the seaside.

'Wind down the windows,' said Great Auntie Dot. 'It's like an oven in here.'

Great Auntie Dot's car was very old-fashioned.

'Is it a Victorian car?' asked Maxine.

'Not quite that old,' laughed Great Auntie Dot. 'People like us didn't have cars in Victorian times. But some things never change. I bet that the Victorians made sandcastles just as we still do.'

'Let's make a really big one!' said Minnie.

'A gigantic one!' said Maxine.

The sand was hot and when Minnie walked over it towards the sea, her toes sank softly into it with each step, leaving footprints to show where she'd been.

When she got to the sea, Minnie paddled and watched the water coming and going, coming and going over her feet until she began to feel dizzy.

'Come on, Min!' shouted Maxine. 'We need the water to make the sand stick!' Minnie scooped a bucket-full of seawater and hurried back up the beach to Maxine.

'I've got shells and some seaweed for making a garden for the castle,' said Maxine. She was digging deep in a circle and piling the sand in the middle of it. 'That pile will be the castle and the ditch will be a moat all around it.'

'What's the moat for?' asked Minnie.

'To keep out the enemies,' said Maxine. She patted the sides of the castle with her spade. Then she leant close to Minnie. 'Maybe your dad lives in a castle like this?'

They made people for the castle out of ice lolly sticks with faces drawn on them with Minnie's mum's pen. 'Just think,' whispered Maxine. 'You might have a real prince and princess brother and sister living in a castle somewhere, Min!'

Minnie looked at the stiff little stick people living in the sand castle with no windows and the sea coming to wash it all away. Suddenly she stood up and stomped off over the sand.

'Where are you going, Min?' asked Maxine.

'Nowhere,' said Minnie. 'Leave me alone.'

Minnie walked on to the edge of the sea and she kicked and kicked the water sparkling into the sunshine. Then an arm hugged around her. It was her mum.

'Minnie, love, what's the matter?'

'Everything's the matter!' said Minnie. She kicked the water again. 'You *still* haven't told me about my dad and Maxine keeps making things up. She thinks that I'm somebody special. She thinks my dad is a king or something and I'm going to go and live in a castle with a family I don't know. She thinks . . .'

Minnie's mum said, 'I think its high time that you heard the real story of Minnie Brown. Come on, let's walk and I'll tell it to you.'

'What about the others?' asked Minnie.

'They can spare us for a few minutes. This story is just for you.' Minnie slipped her hand into her mum's.

'How does it begin?' she asked.

'Once upon a time there was a little girl called Carol. One day, Carol saw a new boy arrive at her school. He was from a children's home. The boy didn't have any mother or father or brothers or sisters. Some of the other children at school teased the boy because he was small and shy and he didn't have anybody to stick up for him. Carol didn't think that was fair, so she shouted at the bullies to leave the new boy alone.'

'That was brave of her,' said Minnie.

'Not really because she didn't stop and think about it. She was so angry,' said Minnie's mum. 'Anyway, Carol and the boy got talking and they found that they lived near to each other and they liked doing lots of the same kind of things. They became friends.'

'Was Carol you?' asked Minnie.

'That's right.'

'And what was the boy's name?'

'His name was David Brown.'

Minnie squeezed her mum's hand hard. 'Was he my dad?' she asked, and her mother nodded.

'What happened?'

'Well, Carol and David went all through school as best friends. Then David went to university and Carol went to college, and they were still best friends. They wrote each other letters and met up together in the holidays. Then one day David came home from university when it wasn't a holiday. He knocked on Carol's door and he said he had something important that he wanted to tell her.'

'Was it that he loved her?' asked Minnie, but her mother shook her head.

'No. I'm afraid that David had some very terrible news, Min. He told Carol that he was very ill and that it wouldn't be long before he would die.'

'Oh, no!'

'Yes,' said Minnie's mum.

'What did they do?'

'David borrowed a friend's car and he drove Carol to the seaside and they

walked along the beach and talked about everything.'

'Like we are now?' asked Minnie.

'Yes. And as they walked and talked they found something.'

'Treasure?'

'They found that they weren't just best friends after all. They found that they loved each other very much. The found that they wanted to spend every moment of the time that David had left, together.'

'So they got married?'

'We married as soon as we could. And we lived together in a little house that we rented and we were very happy. But before we had been married for a year, David died.'

Minnie swallowed hard, then asked, 'Did he leave you anything to remember him by, like Great Auntie Dot's granny leaving her the locket?'

Minnie's mum smiled. 'He left me something much better than a locket, Min. He left me you.'

'Did he ever meet me?'

'You were born after he died,' said her mum. 'But he knew that you were growing inside me. He loved you. And he gave you something too.'

'What?'

'He gave you your name, Minnie. He said that you were a miniature of the two of us. So, you see, Min, you really are very special. Maxine was right about that.'

'But I'm glad I'm not a princess,' said Minnie.

'Oh, so am I,' smiled her mum. 'Now we'd better get back and help with that castle.'

'Mum?' said Minnie. 'Can I stick another bit of paper to my family tree and put my dad's name there?'

'I'll help you do it,' said mum.

When Great Auntie Dot left next morning, she told Minnie, 'I'd like you to keep the locket with your great-great-granny's photograph in it, Minnie. There's room on the other side of it for another picture too, if you've got a special one.'

Minnie's mum found a tiny

photograph of David Brown when he was a little boy and Minnie put it carefully into the locket. She showed it to Maxine.

'That's my dad,' she said.

'He looks nice,' said Maxine.

'He was,' said Minnie. 'He and Mum were best friends.'

'Like us?' said Maxine.

'Yes,' said Minnie. 'Let's be best friends for always.'

'Yes, let's,' said Maxine.